UEA PUBLISHING PROJECT
NORWICH

KYOKO
YOSHIDA

SPRING
SLEEPERS

Spring Sleepers
Kyoko Yoshida

First published by
Strangers Press, Norwich, 2017
part of UEA Publishing Project

Distributed by
NBN International

Printed by
Swallowtail Print, Norwich

An early version of "Spring Sleepers" appeared in the Spring 1998 issue of the Alabama Literary Review

Series editors
David Karashima
Elmer Luke

Editorial team
Kate Griffin
Nathan Hamilton
Philip Langeskov

Cover design and typesetting
Nigel Aono-Billson
Glen Robinson

ISBN-13: 978-1911343035

FSC
www.fsc.org
RECYCLED
Paper made from recycled material
FSC® C113523

FOREWORD

When I was a teenager, I sometimes had the experience of coming back still excited from a party or dance, and then of lying in bed imagining I was still at the event. I would go over conversations I had had or imagine conversations I might have had but didn't. At some point, I would slide into sleep only to be awoken to hear my own voice keeping up its side of the conversation in the dark. I often experienced a moment of profound confusion, with part of me still at the party and another part knowing I was lying in darkness somewhere – but not, at least for an instant, sure where.

One of the great things about Kyoko Yoshida's 'Spring Sleepers' is how it operates in that moment of overlapped realities, refusing to be either completely real or completely a dream, and keeps you suspended in that ambiguity. If you're an insomniac – and who isn't, considering the state of the world these days? – you'll feel on a subdermal level how Yoshida manages to capture that feeling of not knowing whether you're awake or asleep, of stumbling through an odd sort of half-life in which you can no longer determine what is and isn't real. She captures the way you can go from feeling like you have endless energy and that you'll never need to sleep ever again to the feeling that, wait, maybe I just blacked out for a moment there: what did I miss? What was my body doing while I was…where was I exactly?

As insomniacs, we come to ourselves knowing that our lips have just moved, made some sort of utterance, but are unsure what that utterance was, unsure why people are looking at us with expectant and slightly nervous expressions, waiting for us to go on.

One of the nice things about the title story in this chapbook is the way such questions are displaced from the main character Yuki to us as readers. We begin to doubt our own attentiveness, our own relation to what the text depicts, and also begin to mistrust everything. The story makes us experience the uncanny. From one perspective, there's a long tradition of Japanese literature that does just that (Haruki Murakami, for instance). And yet, Yoshida, as someone who writes in both English and Japanese, brings an awareness not only of that tradition but of the tradition of contemporary American fabulism (Kelly Link, George Saunders). What interests me as a writer is the way that the piece seems to be engaged in a conversation between those two traditions, making one think at moments of one and at others of the other, of Yoko Ogawa, say, at one instant and of Paul La Farge at another.

Indeed, Yoshida subtly passes back and forth between one lens and the other, suggesting that literature is less a national enterprise and more a productive interchange between genres, traditions, languages, and cultures. But above all, hers is the kind of work that leaves you off balance, that continues to eat away at you long after you've finished the story.

So, prepare to be eaten.

BRIAN EVENSON

Spring sleepers never see the dawn,
hearing occasional singing of birds.

Meng Haoran
Tang dynasty poet

SPRING
AWAKENING

The eel spends seven years in a narrow compartment of a tube buried in the mud. As the years pass, the sludge swirls upward and streaks of light reach to the murk at the bottom of the lake where the tube sits. That's how the eel knows time is passing. When a seventh spring comes, the eel inches out of the tube and lies on the mud quietly. Or rather, it floats just above the mud, feeling fuzzy swishes of the mire brushing against its scaled soft white belly. It hears a mockingbird mimicking someone whistling a popular song from seven years ago. It listens to the song for a day and then slithers back into the tube.

The most fearsome part of the sickness of insomnia was not the impossibility of sleeping, for the body did not feel any fatigue at all, but its inexorable evolution toward a more critical manifestation: a loss of memory.

Gabriel Garcia Marquez
One Hundred Years of Solitude

SPRING
SLEEPERS

15

Spring had come. Spring, when one would doze in gentle late morning light streaming through gauze curtains. The cherry blossom petals were falling like snow, covering the ponds, meadows, streets. The hills wore the blush of pink. In the distance, the skyline of mountains was blurred by the powder-fine loess brought by winds from the Gobi, but nearer, there was the smell of ashes, mist, violets under clover, and the Chinese milk vetch. The soil was soft, warm, and damp.

The club's waiters in white Mao jackets had opened the windows halfway to allow in the fresh air, and occasional flurries of petals swirled into the smoking room. The wind was still chilly. Warm plum wine and the last hot sake of the year were served in Portuguese hand-blown glasses.

Conversation was quiet, voices low, punctuated by the clinking of the glasses.

The smoke of cigars mingled in the air, rising up to the balcony, exposing the path of the afternoon sunlight.

Up on the mezzanine were two young men seated in rosewood chairs. Yuki was sipping some orange juice through a blue-striped straw, as Haru licked the rim of his martini glass. He daintily placed the glass on the side table, and leaned against the rail to listen in on the gentlemen downstairs.

The conversation was about insomnia. The gentlemen were boasting about how little they slept.

Tucking strands of hair over his pretty face behind his ear, Haru turned back to Yuki and pulled a finely latticed fan out of his purple kimono sleeve. He slowly spread the fan open in front of his heart. His movement was so fluid that Yuki did not notice the fan until the scent of sandalwood tickled his nostrils. Yuki unbuttoned the collar of his dress shirt. The perfumes of Caribbean tobacco and the sandalwood were too much.

"I haven't slept for several days. I suffer from a nausea around midnight that prevents me from sleeping," Haru said in mild complaint.

"Oh well," Yuki said, shrugging. "Don't worry, I haven't slept for two months and I've been feeling great."

"Two months?" Haru raised his right eyebrow, as his coral-ringed hand dangled, still holding the fan. He looked at Yuki – *this plain, large-boned, simple-minded, young bore hadn't slept for two months?* It was impossible to believe that he was sensitive enough or had enough concerns to be sleepless.

"I don't mind," Yuki said cheerfully, "as long as I feel fine. In fact, I feel better nowadays."

Haru spread open his fan again, this time in front of his soft, narrow face, as he recoiled from Yuki. "You may want to stay away from me, Yuki," he said in a whisper that seemed at least tender. "You'd better see your doctor. Now excuse me, but I have an appointment with my *sangen* teacher." Then he got up and left.

ZZZ

"You have *genuine insomnia*."

At last Dr. Gotow spoke, the next morning, after peeping into Yuki's pupils, knocking his chest, feeling his belly, hammering his knees, sniffing his urine, et cetera.

"It infects by physical contact. Any definitive cure is yet to be discovered. All I can do for you is to introduce you to a sanatorium. Go there. But remember: do not touch anyone."

The doctor slipped his fingers into a pair of latex gloves and handed a piece of paper to Yuki. It was a round-trip plane ticket perforated down the middle, dividing it into AWAY and HOME. On the reverse was an advertisement for a sheep-counting machine.

Yuki thanked Dr. Gotow and gathered his things. The doctor saw him to the door.

ZZZ

If you are to spend time in a sanatorium, you need summer clothes, for it is sure to be located in a warm climate. Yuki gazed into the empty suitcase spread on his bed as he conjured images of convalescence.

Sunshine but cool under the green shades. Breeze from mountains, zephyr from the sea. Translucent lakes. Stars in the evening sky. Loneliness. Harmless exchanges with strangers. Sunbathing in early morning in his nightshirt. A long walk along a winding path in pinewoods. The lapping of waves.

He needed a pair of Turkish leather slippers, a pair of linen pants, a Panama hat, a polo shirt, sunscreen, a long, long sleeping shirt, and books to read for one thousand and one nights without sleep.

Yuki lined up the items neatly on the edge of his bed. Then he walked around the bedroom for a while before adding a light woolen cardigan just in case.

After a lunch of toast with butter and marmalade and a cup of tea, he told his dead grandfather's butler, Samukawa, that he was going to visit his friend in the South who had just lost his wife and needed company to share her memories.

"I won't be back for a while. Take care, Samukawa."

Yuki wanted to pat Samukawa's shoulder, but he refrained.

Yuki left by the front door, seen off by two housemaids – who had worked so long for the family that they looked identical – and three borzois, and Samukawa. His mind was clear, his footsteps light, and his heart merry. It was strange to think that he was heading to a sanatorium.

The airport was rather empty. It was a weekday. As Yuki checked in, a compact woman in a tight navy uniform slid out from behind the counter.

"Mr. Minami? How nice to meet you! My name is Barbra. Dr. Gotow asked me to attend to you on board. Will you please follow me? Oh, you must carry your suitcase with you directly to the aircraft."

To catch up with swift-walking Barbra, Yuki had to run while pulling his suitcase. He caught his foot on it several times. Barbra kept skating effortlessly, never turning back to see how he was doing. Yuki wiped his forehead, panting.

Barbra stood waiting for him at gate Q49. Without delay, she opened the gate, a smile carved on the lower part of her face. Yuki followed her into a jumbo jet. There was no one else inside. Barbra secured the door, and the aircraft was immediately in motion.

"Don't you have any other passengers?"

"No," Barbra replied merrily. "This aircraft is chartered specially for you, sir."

Barbra looked at Yuki, whose face froze at this information.

"Oh my," she said, "didn't you know that?"

Yuki said nothing, and Barbra disappeared into the cabin galley.

As Yuki fell into his seat, his suitcase, which was too bulky to store in the overhead bin, began to slide. By the time Yuki stood up to grab it, it was rolling, roaring down the aisle. The plane lifted off the ground, Yuki lost his balance, and he and his suitcase tumbled down the aisle to the stern restroom. Barbra poked her head out from the galley curtain, smiled professionally, and ducked her head back in. Yuki crawled back to his seat, leaving the suitcase behind. He rubbed his limbs and his head, feeling a bump rising.

Barbra reappeared from the galley in a white chef's outfit with a tall hat. Freshly powdered, she cat-walked toward Yuki and handed him a menu. A meal on board is the highlight of a flight, and Yuki's mouth watered as he opened the menu. It was written, however, in wriggling letters he had never seen before. He guessed, from the structure of the menu, that the meal consisted of six courses. That was all he could guess. Yuki gazed at the strange letters, of which he most admired one that was flowery, a composition of four circles, or rather four balloons tied together at the centre, like a rose, or a cross.

Barbra came back pushing the beverage cart. Yuki asked for a glass of orange juice. Barbra cut three oranges into halves and squeezed them in front of him. She served the juice to him in a glass. A narrow plastic tube with blue stripes stuck out of the glass. Yuki began to stare at the tube intensely. He squeezed it gently, pulled it out, and laid it on the tray.

Yuki couldn't help staring at it. It prevented him from drinking the juice. To his great relief, Barbra picked it up from the tray, put it into her breast pocket, and walked away. Yuki and his orange juice were left behind. He brought the glass to his lips and drained it.

The meal was fine, but it did not make him drowsy. Yuki sat upright in the seat, staring at the stars outside the window. Before long, Barbra returned wearing a pink negligee, her hair in curlers, holding a ruffled pillow under her arm.

"Good night, sir." She rubbed her eyes, still keeping her smile. After informing Yuki that audiovisual entertainment would be available to him after breakfast, she retired into the rear of the cabin.

Yuki wanted to ask her how many hours they would fly, where they were heading, and, if it was not a direct flight, where and when they would stop. At least he could ask when the breakfast would be served. But he always had trouble asking for such information casually. Before he could compose himself, the low vibration of her snore trailed down the aisle from the cabin to his seat.

ZZZ

John Huston's *Moby-Dick* was the only movie available. When the credits appeared on the twelve monitors for the twelfth time, Yuki politely asked Barbra (now in her movie theatre apparel – a bowling shirt over a long-sleeve T-shirt smelling of butter) if she could turn off the monitor. Barbra obliged him. Yuki patiently waited for the moment the sand would get into his unblinking eyes. The sandman did not come. Yuki folded his arms and lay them on the tray and rested his head on them. He turned his head to the side, and looked through the window. He saw no light. The aircraft was chasing the night. It was always in the dark hemisphere. The waning moon and glittering stars led the plane. There was no indication of time passing.

By the time he saw the city lights for the first time, after what seemed like three days' sitting, every fibre of his muscles was aching.

The city was on the water – whether a river, a lake, or the sea, he could not tell.

Among the silhouettes of buildings crammed along the shore, smokestacks spewed thick white columns of smoke into a leaden atmosphere. The amber street lamps glimmered in the dark. It was snowing.

As the plane approached closer, more buildings came into view. Some of them had to have been built a long time ago. The water the city was on appeared black and thick. It did not look liquid.

Now the plane was low enough for Yuki to examine the details of the town.

Among tall stone buildings were pinnacles of churches, or of former churches, the crosses replaced with lightning rods. The plane flew over a large bridge (or viaduct?) from which rose a clock tower with four faces, lit by fluorescent lights.

As the plane landed softly, Yuki felt as if he heard the clocks peal the eleventh hour. He knew it was his hallucination. Still he was sure he sensed the silent vibration.

Just then his suitcase slid back to his side.

Descending the stairs, Yuki was buffeted by a gust of wind that pelted him with sleet. Yuki clung to the railing, hugging his suitcase. The sleet felt like needles piercing his soft skin. This is not a place for a sanatorium, he told himself. This is no place for recuperation. Yuki turned around and looked up: farewell-dressed Barbra was smiling, bidding him goodbye with a lacy handkerchief. He turned around and looked down: a small mole of a man with a brown knit cap was waiting at the foot of the stairs. Beside him was a brick-coloured Buick. Yuki found soon later that half the brick colour was rust. The man spoke Yuki's name. Before Yuki could reply, he slipped, his buttocks landing on the snow-covered tarmac. It was not a soft landing. The mole man held out his hand. "Mr. Minami. I will take you to the clinic."

Yuki waved off the hand of help.

"Thank you, but you shouldn't touch me."

zzz

Before Yuki's hand reached the knob, the door banged open in his face.

He squatted down on the porch covering his nose with his hands.

"Here you are!"

The booming voice came from above Yuki's head.

"What are you doing sitting down there? Get up and come on in! I've been waiting for you, Mr. Minami. I'm your doctor! I am Dr. Springman! Nice to meet you! Oops, we don't shake hands! Dr. Gotow set out everything right for you!"

The clinic had the look of an elementary school library with all the colourful books on the shelves and posters on the wall and cards scattered around on the floor. A mobile of papier-mâché tropical fish was hanging above the doctor's yellow plastic desk, where he had been folding paper cranes. The tiny cranes in different colours were perched in line and staring at Yuki, who was wondering why the mobile kept in motion even though there was no wind.

As Dr. Springman spoke, Yuki noticed steam rising from the doctor's shiny forehead, radiating heat, the by-product of his enthusiastic gestures, which generated an updraft, which gave the fish mobile motion.

While Yuki was absorbed in this thermodynamic phenomenon, Dr. Springman boasted about his splendid career, his arms going up and down. He got Yuki's attention when he brought out a narrow plastic tube and removed it from its wrapping of thin paper.

"Now, what is this?"

Yuki became suddenly perplexed. He had never seen such a thing before. He agonised. He started to knock his head. The doctor threw the thing away and told him to forget it, giggled to himself, mumbling, "Anyway, you've forgotten already," then announced solemnly that Yuki appeared to be suffering from *genuine insomnia*. The doctor was totally bewildered by this new patient. Waving his arms wildly, he said that this was a very rare disease and he had seen it only in a novel. He explained the first symptoms of *genuine insomnia*: after a couple of wakeful months, you forget what a "straw" is (at this word, Yuki became even more restless). That was then followed by forgetting what was a "chair," a "suitcase," a "sanatorium," a "clip," "sunscreen," a "watch," a "toothbrush," and on and on and on. He then said that there was nothing he could do to bring back lost memory of this kind as he could with an amnesiac.

"So forget the forgotten," he said. "Let's do something about the remains of the memory which you are liable to lose in the future. Otherwise, the virus just continues to erase your memory until it whites your brain out entirely. Recently, I succeeded in developing a revolutionary method to maintain your memory. I call it *PrintinMnemonics*–"

Before Dr. Springman went on, Yuki could not help speaking up: "Doctor. I want to sleep. I came here to sleep."

The doctor stopped talking and waving his arms and stared at this poor patient as if he were a strange creature.

"Sleeplessness causes no harm to your health. In fact, the longer you've been awake, the better you feel."

Yuki nodded.

"See? Imagine how many people wish to be like you in this competitive world." And the doctor sighed dramatically.

"But I want to sleep. Dr. Gotow told me there is a sanatorium where I will be able to sleep."

Dr. Springman became irritated because he was just about to talk about it. The sanatorium was in the castle on Mount Fumi, located at the north end of the city.

"But it is no use," he said. "Because you will completely forget the word sanatorium before you reach there. So there is no way you can get to the sanatorium."

Yuki appeared unsatisfied.

The doctor took a deep breath. "If you want to sleep so badly, you may try the medication I developed. This amazing tablet contains chloroplast as an active ingredient that transforms the solar energy into the somnus energy. The brighter the sun, the better you sleep. You'll sleep soundly as long as the sun shines upon you. You must not forget to put on sunscreen before you fall asleep otherwise you'll be burnt to a crisp. It works perfectly until you forget the word sunscreen, which comes next to -"

Yuki said *nothankyou* for the medicine and left the clinic, heading north to the sanatorium. The mountain lay far away.

ZZZ

The traffic signal turned green. People started to move forward like a herd of cattle. Yuki missed the start and, pushed by those behind, tripped. A man with sunglasses held Yuki by his arm, keeping him from falling. The man smelt of ashes.

"Thank you," said Yuki. "But you'd better not touch me."

"His fleece was as white as snow," the man responded, his slender gold-ringed hands not letting go of Yuki's upper arm. Yuki looked up at his face, but the sunglasses were too dark to see the man's eyes. The man was wearing a tuxedo with a ruffled shirt despite the hour of day.

"That little lamb I am talking about," he whispered. This time he bent his head down so that Yuki could see his eyes through the space between his nose and sunglasses. Yuki was startled at the man's turquoise eyes smiling at him. "Sleep, little one, go to sleep," the man began to sing.

"So peaceful bird and the sheep...," Yuki took over the lullaby lyrics.

"Yes! And his fleece was white as..."

"Snow, that is my name," Yuki said awkwardly.

On hearing this, the man broke into a wide flowery smile.

"So you *are* the one to count the lambs to infinity," he said, pulling Yuki up with a jerk. He made a gesture to follow, and started to walk away. Yuki stood where he was. After several steps, the man had to turn back to Yuki. "Come on," he said. "Follow me."

Yuki followed him.

The man walked into alleys with his hands in his pockets. He made sudden turns. Every so often, the man looked around, apparently watching for shadows. After seven or eight blocks, he opened a door to a greasy diner.

The man walked straight into the kitchen. Yuki hesitated to follow him. Soon the smoke and steam shrouded the man's figure, and Yuki hurried into the kitchen in order not to lose the man's lead. Through the long, narrow kitchen, the two walked side by side.

At the other end of the kitchen, the man pushed the door open, and then they were in a dark, empty hall. Candlelit, it appeared like a church, but the room did not bear any religious sign. Yuki shivered and remained standing.

"Have a seat," the man said, still wearing his sunglasses.

Half listening, Yuki turned his head about, looking around the hall with his mouth slightly open. He gazed down at the man in the chair.

"Okay. Never mind." The man shrugged. He lifted his hand, extending it within reach of Yuki's hand, expectant. Yuki looked at the hand and then the man.

"My name is Mary," the man said. "And pal, you're Snow? You're my partner from South?" Mary's right hand was still in the air, waiting to be shaken.

"What partner?" Yuki's voice came out almost angry. A moment later, he added, "Don't touch me."

Mary dropped his hand. "Remember this?" he asked Yuki, pulling out a small pin from his pocket. It was a miniature crusader shield in ultramarine enamel with a vermilion cross. Under the cross were the letters "S.S."

Yuki bent over to inspect the pin closely. "It's a Sunday school pin. I remember that. They gave one to me when I was nine."

"No," Mary said, "It's a secret spy pin. Don't you *remember*, pal?"

Yuki was not sure.

"I'm not a spy." That was all he could say.

"Everybody says so," Mary replied.

"I am an invalid. I came here for medical treatment."

"If you are a genuine spy, you must play sick really well." Mary rubbed his hands. "You'll do an excellent job if you pair with me."

Yuki felt giddy.

"I must go," he said.

"Yes. Good spies know when to leave. Remember, we will manoeuvre separately. This is the first and the last contact between us. Good luck, and watch out for the shadows."

Mary put some small change on the wooden table in the hall, gave Yuki a casual salute, and left the hall from the front door.

Yuki headed north again.

ZZZ

On the bridge, a tall man and a small boy were placing small glass bottles of various sizes on the tattered rug spread on the ground. They might have been picked out of trash cans.

The tall man had hip-length grey hair pulled into a ponytail and held together. The sleeves of his white lab coat were too short for his long bony arms. The elbows were threadbare. On his back was a scribble in red: *CHEMISTORY*.

“Born unwise, die wise,” he yelled in a ringing, deep voice, like a maestro on stage. “At last! A medicine to cure stupidity! The medicine for fools!”

“Medicine for fools,” the boy echoed feebly, his legs dangling over the parapet. He was dressed better than his boss, in his black schoolboy uniform and a hat. His cheeks were apple red, small lips berry purple. He was blowing white breath on his frostbitten hands, shivering.

“Master,” the boy whimpered, “I’m freezing. Hungry, too. Nobody buys the thing. Let’s go home.”

The man called Master cast a stern glance at the poor boy before he threw himself in front of a pale man coming down the bridge in summer clothes.

“Good afternoon, sir!” he shouted. “I suppose you are a novelist!”

Yuki froze, staring at this scraggy man. It took him a moment to say no.

“But you are a storyteller, am I right?”

“No. I…”

“You may call me Master.”

“Mm, Master, I’m not a…”

“I have a great secret of novel autoproduction that I will sell you!” Master proclaimed, standing with his chin pointed upward.

Yuki gave up claiming his identity. Or denying it. He had learned to give up much quickly. The boy on the parapet smirked.

“Time is Father, Place is Mother, and their child is a Story!” Master jumped onto the parapet and started to sway. “As Time passes by, Place becomes pregnant. Combinations are endless. A place of wilderness; a time of betrayal. A place of fraud; a time of river. A place of water; a time of evolution. A place of crocuses; a time of ashes. A place of tears; a time of mandarin orange. A place of snow; a time of lambs.”

“A place of needles,” Yuki murmured.

“There you go! You are getting at it. A time of Manila envelope.”

“A place of cat and a time of dog,” the boy added.

“Marriage of Time and Place. That is the secret,” said the man.

“But Master,” Yuki interrupted. “Where are the characters? Where are human beings in the story?”

“Human beings?” The man’s voice had turned harsh suddenly. He jumped off the parapet onto the bridge. “Who cares about them? They are everywhere, no matter how hard you try to get rid of them. We didn’t ask them to be *there* and *then*, but here they are to mess up everything. Oh, they are so helpless, don’t you agree? Didn’t you learn the first thing at school that people have nothing to do with Time and Place?”

“But Master…”

“Stop the but. And quit calling me Master! I ain’t no teacher, no employer, no captain, no leader, no father, no heir, no owner, no keeper, no bartender of yours.”

The man breathed heavily, heaving. His young disciple giggled.

“But Master, I need no novel autoproduction. I just want to cure my insomnia.”

“I have a fine medicine for you.” The *former* Master stuck his forefinger up and reached into his pocket to pull out a small blue glass bottle. “These amazing tablets contain chloroplast as an active ingredient to transform the solar energy into the somnus energy, and – ”

Yuki said *nothankyou* politely.

“Oh, you don’t want that? Well, then I can teach you a marvelous method to keep your memory fresh as long as possible. The method is…”

“…*PrintinMnemonics*.” Master-turned-chemist and Yuki had spoken at the same time.

“You know it?”

“Just the name,” Yuki said.

“It is quite simple. Remember your teachers made you recite poems when you were little? You learnt not by *heart*; you learnt by *mouth*.”

This time, the chemist raised his forefinger slowly like a symphony conductor, touching his lower lip. Then he pointed to Yuki’s full mouth as if to cast a spell on Yuki, who stood still, mesmerised.

The chemist started slowly: “Repeat a word until it becomes your mouth’s memory, instead of your heart’s. Repeat it again and again so that your mercurial memory remains upon your lips, not in your floating mind.” He jumped onto the parapet and began a mincing dance.

“Feet, stamp!” he shouted, waving his arms at Yuki and the boy, cueing them to repeat after him.

“Feet. Stamp,” they repeated in limp unison.

“Eyes, look!” The chemist shouted, rolling his eyes.

“Eyes. Look.”

“Ears, listen.” The chemist closed his eyes.

“Ears. Listen.” The boy began to clap his hands with joy.

“Stars, shine!” Venus appeared as he waved to the dusky sky.

“Stars. Shine.”

“Dog, run!” A dog materialised, trotting across the bridge.

"Dog. Run."

"Shadow, chase." A long stretch of silhouette chased the dog.

"Shadow. Chase."

"Snow, freeze."

"Snow. Freeze." The chemist sneezed into the icy air.

"I, repeat."

"I. Repeat."

"Song, sing."

"Song. Sing." A shrill whistle came from the farther end of the bridge. Hurried footsteps followed.

"Police! Police!" a voice cried,

"Who's selling drugs here?" A different voice this time.

"Police!"

The chemist and his disciple quickly wrapped up their bottles in the rug and were gone.

ZZZ

Alone, Yuki stood repeating the words. Then he started heading north, reciting and tottering.

Road Lead

Sun Light

Moon Reflect

River Flow

Wind Blow

zzz

The world had had three dimensions. The world had been crammed with details: shapes, colours, lights, shades, odours, soundwaves, sandwiches, atmospheres, temperatures. When his eyes opened, they had sucked in an orange dog trotting by the ditch hemmed with veronica, patches of grey on an abandoned farm house, anxious whispers of willows swinging in the damp gale, tanned, bare feet of a boy under the tree gazing into a tin bucket, in which water reflected his face and crayfish scratched, a smile on an old woman through the frosted glass. He had been choked by nouns and adjectives, verbs and adverbs, exclamations and more nouns and even more adjectives. So many flower names to remember and so many constellations to chase after.

Being sleepless was as if walking through dark woods – like a brother and a sister left in the black forest – scattering pieces of bread behind or dropping torn and crumpled pages of his memory. Birds and goats followed him silently, munching on the crumbs and scraps. There was a constant rustle of sand as he walked. He was shouldering a sandbag. It had an invisible hole. As he walked, the burden became lighter. He was liberating the past as he walked. Or was the past fleeing him as it pushed him through the woods? When he passed through the woods after the bridge, another world opened up. The liquefied world, the disassembled world of pieces and fragments in bold lines and vivid colours. Against the backdrop of flat buildings and houses played a puppet show of paper-cut dogs and people. There was no distance to the stars. They stuck flat on the hard blackboard of night. There was no distance, but they were unreachable. The city was now composed of lines and segments, angles and curves. Triangles, circles, squares. The world was now two-dimensional, made of a series of disconnected planes hung vertically from the heavenly ceiling.

During the days, he was nervous. Just the thought of another sleepless night burned him with anxiety. The anxiety of monotony. At night, he was bored. Night was forever. It was solid, unbreakable. Counting the nights he walked through and imagining more sleepless nights, he found the prospect of thousands of boring nights pathetically boring.

ZZZ

The cheer and chatter of children turned the corner of the flat building. Short paper-cut figures surged against him and onto the bridge. They were made of circles, triangles, and rectangles. All were identical. They were stick people. Each had a small mouth, perfectly round, constantly moving like a goldfish. They screamed:

Fireworks! Fireworks! Fireworks in winter!

It was still snowing. The wind was gone. The fluffy snow had turned into powder.

Children came in droves. There had to be hundreds of stick children hidden behind the flat building. A fountain of stick children. Maybe they were born there. They raced with each other over the bridge. They surely did not want to miss the fireworks. Their voices and steps died away.

It was quiet again. When he resumed walking, he heard a sob.

He found a circle sticking out from behind the flat building. It was a head of a paper-cut child. It was sobbing.

He asked it what the matter was.

It said to him, my mama doesn't let me go to the fireworks.

Because its family was poor and could not afford a coat for it to go out on a freezing night. It thought of the bursts, the bangs, the flowers of light, the laughter it could never share with its stick friends. Crystal marbles dropped out of a pair of round eyes. It wanted to go to the fireworks so badly.

He told the stick child to take his cardigan. It hesitated. The child's cheeks shone, but it shook its circle head. He pulled off his cardigan. Underneath was a polo shirt. He put the cardigan on the stick child. The sleeves dangled from the stick child's hands. He knelt and buttoned up the cardigan for the stick child. Its face brightened. He patted its tummy. It giggled.

The stick child thanked him and ran away. As it passed the bridge, it turned back to him three times before the arch of the bridge hid its figure.

He sat on the shoulder of the street. A dog came up to him and sniffed his legs. Powdery snow melted on his bare arms. He sneezed. The dog was scared off.

The stick child came back. He knew it was that particular stick child because it wore his cardigan. The ends of the sleeves swung as the stick child ran.

It ran pit-a-pat toward him.

It poked out its arms to him. There was a small red ball in the child's hands. It must be an apple. The ball was not a perfect sphere. It had a dent. The stick child must have had a bite.

The paper child told him that the apple was all it could offer him. He took the apple. The child was delighted. It thanked him again and ran away. It turned back to him and waved at him three times before the arch of the bridge hid its figure.

He squatted on the street. He held the red ball in his hands. He sniffed at it.

It smelt like spring. He took a bite and threw up at once. It was a bitter apple. He stared at the ball in his hand. He took another bite. This time he did not spew. He ate it all. He enjoyed it slowly. He swallowed all the bitter juice and all the crisp flesh. A core remained. He put it in his pocket. He thought for a while. He started to feel like he could sleep. He closed his eyes. Powdery snow brushed gently against his cheeks. He told himself to sleep but he could not. He felt pathetic. Then he heard thunder. The fireworks had started. He opened his eyes. He saw an enormous red dahlia over the bridge.

On the bridge was a figure. It was not a stick figure as the others, but was a three-dimensional human being. It held fireworks upon its head like a halo. The brightness of the background turned the figure dark. It was approaching him. Slowly.

He looked at it and realised all at once who it was. It was himself. The biggest firework bloomed, followed by a bang. The light illuminated its face. It was his face. It was a woman. She was in a summer dress. She was barefoot. Her limbs were all bone and skin. Her eyes were sunk deep in their sockets. Her gaze cut straight into his head and kneaded his brain. She kept on toward him. She smelt of end.

Another icy flower flashed and stuck to the blackboard of the sky for a moment.

She told him that there had been no such thing as sleep from the beginning.

From the beginning of the world.

He said it wasn't true.

His double sneered at him and said, Then let us assume, as you claim, that there has been such a thing as sleep in this world, if it makes you happy.

Her voice was a direct voice. It reached straight from her mouth to his.

She reached her hands to his neck. They were ice. She pushed him onto the ground.

The double said, You sleep every night. You sleep so well every night that you never notice you are sleeping. You never dream of you sleeping.

She was heavy. She was a rock. He was prone on the ground. He could not breathe. A rock was on his back. He had to say something. He buried his face in the sleet, grabbling for words.

Words.

Many words.

Blah. Blah. Blah.

But he could only say, *No*.

No. No.

Another firework.

He raised his face shouting. She was gone. The bridge was empty. On the blackboard remained the coloured particles of the fireworks.

He knew there had been sleep in his life. He knew he had been sleeping during certain periods of his life. He knew it had been something nice, something precious. But he did not remember why and how it had been precious. His double must be cheating him. She must be stealing his sleep out of his memory.

How did he sleep? If only he remembered how.

He closed his eyes.

A hot bath filled with calamus leaves. His three borzois' tails tapping out a hypnotising beat on the Danzu carpet. A dark bedroom filled with steam. A cup of mint tea with rum. Flannel pajamas. A down comforter. Piles of silk pillows. An arched window to gaze at stars.

He closed his eyes. He remembered none of those. When he closed his eyes, his eyeballs would turn inside and they would show him a muddy emptiness in his skull, not a complete vacuum, but an emptiness half-filled with distorted associations of sounds, letters, and meanings.

He felt he could sleep if he kept his eyes open.

He ran to the airport.

He wanted to go home because home was the place to sleep.

The airport was busy with segments of lines, yields, parallel lines, perpendicular lines, acute angles, obtuse angles, circles bouncing around murmuring a foreign tongue, flamboyant triangles, and shivering squares. Stick figures running about.

He approached the nearest counter.

Home. Home.

Hé said the word again and again. It must have sounded like an old woman mourning over a grave.

Home. Aye. O. Home. Home. Aye.

I need your ticket, a compact stick figure said in a familiar chirpy voice.

He searched his pants pockets for the remaining half of his plane ticket. And his shirt pockets. When he turned his pants pockets inside out, something metallic fell onto the floor. It was a small enamel pin. A moment after, a piece of paper fluttered down and landed beside the pin. It said, HOME.

He stepped forward and bent down.

Somebody yelled at him and knocked him down.

Then the sound.

Crack! Crack! Crack!

As the crowd dispersed screaming, the world restored itself with details.

The furious blast shook the air terminal. The rumble of a stampede. The howling siren of panic. Shrieks of the trampled. A pool of dark liquid spreading under a smiling woman in a navy uniform, lying prone. Among the frenzy, the double clicked her tongue and glided out of the pandemonium. Enter the shouts and whistles of the police squad, then the howling and keening of old women.

Meanwhile the floor was wiped up, the corpse carried out, and the terminal building deserted, except for a young man lying spread-eagled on the cold linoleum floor.

Through the automatic glass door stepped a man dressed in tuxedo. He wore dark sunglasses. He stopped at the man's feet. He removed his sunglasses to take a better look at the still life.

"I told you to watch out for the shadows," Mary said to Yuki. He slowly circled around Yuki's body, murmuring. "You did a good job, pal. You played sick very well. A fabulous invalid you are. A genuine spy." Mary came to a stop next to Yuki's peaceful face. Gently he poked the soft cheek with the toe of his shoe. Yuki's head rolled to the side.

"Hey. Listen. You're awake, right?" He kneeled down and touched his hand to Yuki's face. He lay his ear on Yuki's chest. He closed his turquoise eyes and took a deep breath. Then pushing against the floor with the palm of his hand, he got back up.

"Sweet dreams, pal." He smiled at Yuki and walked away.

Mary left by the automatic glass door.

Snow was falling on the runways, covering the streets, blanketing everything. Yuki remained still, spread-eagled, his eyes closed, hands loosely opened, and mouth slackened.

Soon the snow would white out the sight.

NORWICH: THE CITY
OF WRITING

Sheila Roberts (1937-2009), a novelist from Cape Town and my mentor in Milwaukee, Wisconsin, said to dissertating students in 1999: “You will become like travelling theologians of the medieval times.” It was not an edict sending out pilgrims to the dark wilderness of anti-intellectualism. It was a way to encourage us at a time when the academic job market was shrinking while the number of PhDs was increasing. Literary authors and poets could no longer support themselves simply by writing. Sheila wanted us to recapture our profession, to re-imagine ourselves as migrating writers moving from a colony to a residency, from one fellowship to another, exchanging thoughts with colleagues from different places, and surviving in a world of fast, drastic change. Fifteen years later, as I found myself trading words and ideas with writers at the magnificently renovated medieval Dragon Hall in Norwich, once an entrepôt of the greater North Sea area, I realised that this is what we have actually become – travelling theologians. Sheila herself lived that life in self-exile, like many South African authors. I feel I have lived that life, too, even within Japan, my native country, since I choose to write in a second language.

The 2015 Worlds Literature Festival in Norwich opened with a provocation, in the very modern glass refectory of the 12th century Norwich Cathedral, by Jon Cook, chair of the Arts Council England South East. The year’s theme was “reputation”, and Jon, making reference to London as a literary stock exchange, suggested that art is for the most part produced and traded in such a cultural capital.
Furthermore, he went on, as far as literature was concerned, there is glaring inequality in recognition between works in English and works in non-English. It seemed rather a statement of fact, and these observations, I realised, pertained to me personally – but in unexpected ways: I am a writer who might write in English but in a non-English-speaking country, away from the cultural capital of that country, Japan. The old-world concept of a cultural capital, which I had not

considered for years, is no different there, where your literary reputation depends on publishers and media in Tokyo. But why had I become oblivious to the fact? Perhaps for three reasons: first, because of my debt to the American education system in creative writing, I had somehow come to consider myself as an "American" writer. Second, because I write in a "foreign" language and because I grew up and now live in western Japan, I do not have constant interaction with Tokyo. Finally, despite my peripheral position in "the Republic of Letters," the fact that I write in English has afforded me opportunities to visit and meet with writers in many parts of the world. What is of interest, moreover, is the list of the places I travelled to – Iowa City, Nebraska City, Providence, Hong Kong, Fez, Perth, Bangkok, Jakarta, Singapore, Sydney, Manila, Norwich – all of which would appear miscellaneous compared with the catalogue of the world's illustrious cultural capitals. Inadvertently I had become what my mentor Sheila Roberts had encouraged – a travelling theologian.

This trip to Norwich to participate in Worlds was my second visit to the city. The first time I had spent only a day. This time was both more leisurely and more intense. In a drizzling rain in June, I rolled my suitcase over cobblestone lanes along the River Yare before arriving at the perplexing intersection fronting the Maids Head Hotel. Some complicated construction was ongoing and in order to enter the Tudor-style hotel we had to make a peculiar detour that I never seemed to master. Once inside the Maids Head, the corridors branched off into hooks and nooks, leading the clueless guest to unintended floor levels. It took me a good half-hour to arrive at breakfast the morning after. This physical confusion gave me the sense of feeling lost like a tourist – theology irrelevant.

Writing is deeply rooted in a sense of place. It is a physical knowledge that accumulates in every part of one's body. In literature, culture is built upon the unique personalities of cities and neighbourhoods, and at the same time, the same cities take advantage of, and depend on, their literary histories. London, Paris, St. Petersburg, Baghdad, Shanghai, Kyoto, and New York provide easy examples. And today, there are as well sites of literary experiments that were once targets of mockery and controversy that are now the reference points for a fast-spreading model of education.

Norwich is such a site. And it is two things at once: the most fitting site for today's travelling theologians to meet and share thoughts, securely shut off from worldly disturbances (including that noisy marketplace London); and a new centre of literary production whose reputation is developing not really in competition with London or Tokyo, but in an entirely different way.

One evening, the Worlds participants attended the University of East Anglia's regular student-faculty reading at a local café. The diversity of students at the podium made me envious. These students are Worlds. Soon these faces will represent the literatures in English around the world. The diversity of faculty members astonished me, too – Vesna Goldsworthy, George Szirtes, Amit Chaudhuri, to name just three – and many among them were initially educated in non-English speaking parts of the world. Here in Norwich, I was meeting my long missing fellow travellers.

In particular, I benefited from the mixture of writers, translators, and educators because these three vocations are inseparable in me, and because in "Worlds" of literature, where multiplicity makes the backbone of our belief, we have to portage the vessel of our language across land and from one body of water to another with help. In fact, with a lot of help. A single author's canoe might float and move quickly in native waters, but once the boat has got to ground, its weight could be backbreaking, so several of us, travelling translators and migrating writers all, carry the boat together with slow and heavy tread. The deliberate speed and process of conversation, just to give one example, with the Korean author Han Kang and her interpreter Yunjung Kim and translator Deborah Smith reminded me what we are all trying to express through strange languages within ourselves. Since then I've been following their fearless path: Han Kang's creation of the estranged worlds and Deborah's work of sharing the alienation in another language. And for me, it was a moment of poetic justice come real when the duo won the 2016 Man Booker International Prize – and that the translator's share of portaging was recognized as equally as the author's vision and craft. Tuning in to those inner voices, one has to slow down and listen to the pause between words and the silence between one language and another.

Migrating writers may feel estranged no matter where they go, and yet you may be at home with people who have crossed their own national and language borders – either making your own mother tongue strange or adopting a second or third language. The language of our writing is a strange land where we travel. My itinerary as a writer is unfolding along with the rise and development of the new literary cities like Norwich.

About the Project

Keshiki is a series of chapbooks showcasing the work of some of the most exciting writers working in Japan today, published by Strangers Press, part of the UEA Publishing Project.

Each story is beautifully translated and presented as an individual chapbook, with a design inspired by the text.

Keshiki is a unique collaboration between University of East Anglia, Norwich University of the Arts, and Writers' Centre Norwich, funded by the Nippon Foundation.

Supported by

日本財団
THE NIPPON FOUNDATION

WRITERS' CENTRE NORWICH

UEA
University of East Anglia

NORWICH UNIVERSITY OF THE ARTS

1 —

Time Differences

Yoko Tawada

Translated by Jeffrey Angles

2 —

Friendship for Grown-Ups

Nao-Cola Yamazaki

Translated by Polly Barton

3 —

Spring Sleepers

Kyoko Yoshida

4 —

Mariko/Mariquita

Natsuki Ikezawa

Translated by Alfred Birnbaum

5 —

The Girl Who Is Getting Married

Aoko Matsuda

Translated by Angus Turvill

6 —

At the Edge of the Wood

Masatsugu Ono

Translated by Juliet Winters Carpenter

7 —

Mikumari

Misumi Kubo

Translated by Polly Barton

8 —

The Transparent Labyrinth

Keiichirō Hirano

Translated by Kerim Yasar